S0-BEB-424

The Day I Had to Play with My SISTER

MY FIRST
I Can Read Book®

The Day I Had to Play with My SISTER

story and pictures by
Crosby Bonsall

HarperCollinsPublishers

for Laura

HarperCollins®, ®, and I Can Read Book®
are trademarks of HarperCollins Publishers Inc.

For information address HarperCollins Children's Books,
a division of HarperCollins Publishers,
10 East 53rd Street, New York, NY 10022.

Library of Congress Cataloging-in-Publication Data
Bonsall, Crosby Newell
The day I had to play with my sister / story and pictures by Crosby Bonsall.
p. cm. — (A my first I can read book)
Summary: A young boy becomes very frustrated when he tries to teach his little sister to play hide-and-seek.
ISBN 0-06-028180-4. — ISBN 0-06-028181-2 (lib. bdg.) — ISBN 0-06-444253-5 (pbk.)
[1. Brothers and sisters—Fiction. 2. Hide-and-seek—Fiction. 3. Humorous stories.]
I. Title. II. Series.
PZ7.B64265Day 1999 98-20342
[E]—dc21 CIP
AC

13 SCP 20 19 18 17

Newly illustrated edition

Visit us on the World Wide Web!
http://www.harperchildrens.com

CHAPTER
1

Want to play a game?

You hide.

I will find you.

Okay?

One.
Two.
Three.

Here

I

come.

Ready

or not.

That is not the way
to play the game!

CHAPTER
2

You HIDE, okay?
Hide in back of a tree.

Or hide here, see?

And I will find you, okay?

One, two, three.
Here I come,
ready or not.

I know where you are.

I know. Here!

No, here!

No.

Well, I know where you are.

You are
in the doghouse.

Now, you cut that out!
Hear?

CHAPTER
3

This time I will hide.
You look for me, okay?
You say one, two, three.

You say
here I come,
ready or not. Okay?

Never mind.

I will hide.

You just look for me.

Now, don’t forget
to look
for me.

Get off my lap!

I don’t want
to play with you
anymore.

DISCARD